Summer at Stonehenge

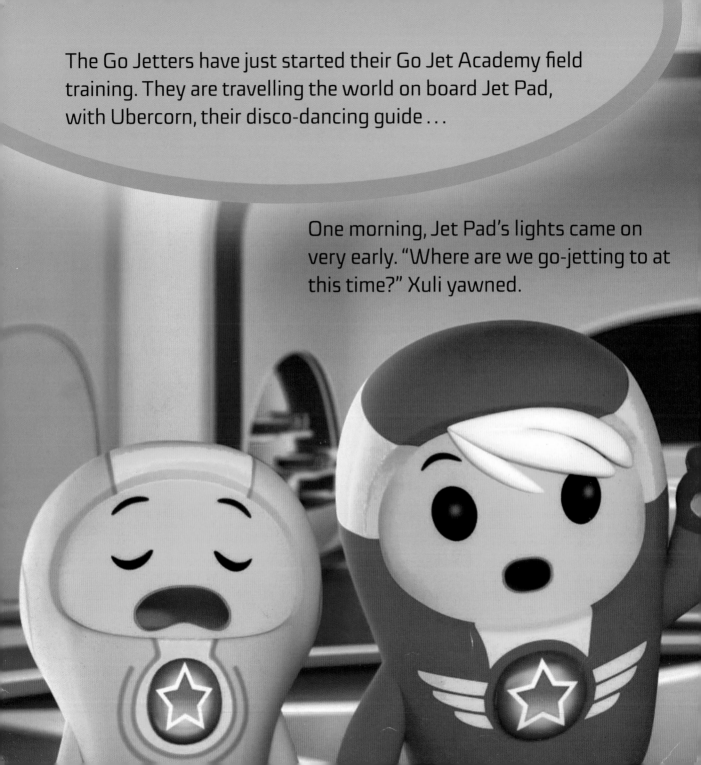

The Go Jetters have just started their Go Jet Academy field training. They are travelling the world on board Jet Pad, with Ubercorn, their disco-dancing guide . . .

One morning, Jet Pad's lights came on very early. "Where are we go-jetting to at this time?" Xuli yawned.

"We're off to Stonehenge in England," Ubercorn replied. "We have to get there before sunrise. So, Go Jetters . . . go!"

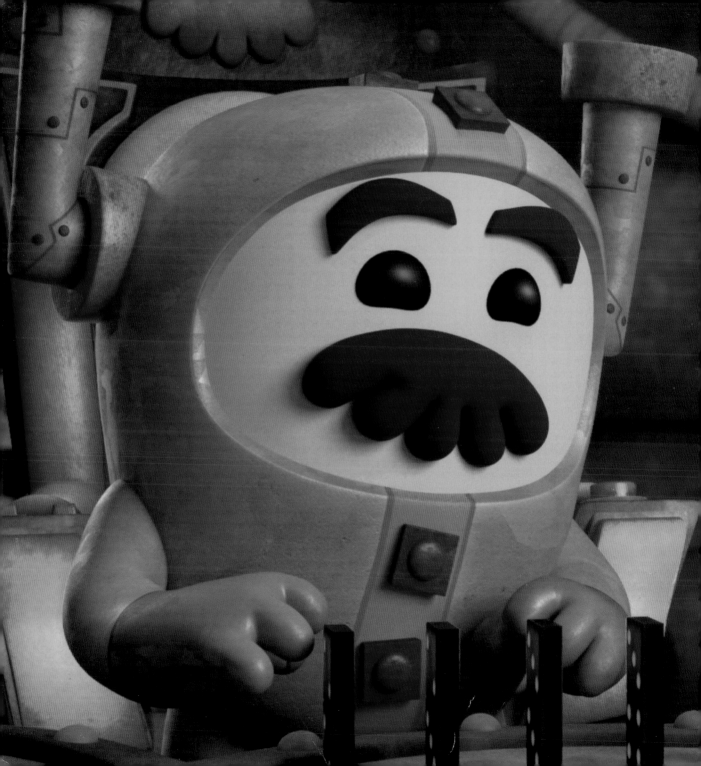

Meanwhile, in Grim HQ, mischievous Grandmaster Glitch was carefully standing up his dominoes.

Just then Jet Pad zoomed past, shaking Glitch's shuttle so hard that all the dominoes fell over!

"Grrr, those No Jetters!" growled Glitch, and he sped after them.

As Jet Pad flew closer to England, the Go Jetters wanted to find out more about Stonehenge.

"Funky Facts time ... hit it!"
Ubercorn sang.

3 "Stonehenge was built in England a long time ago – thousands of years before disco!"

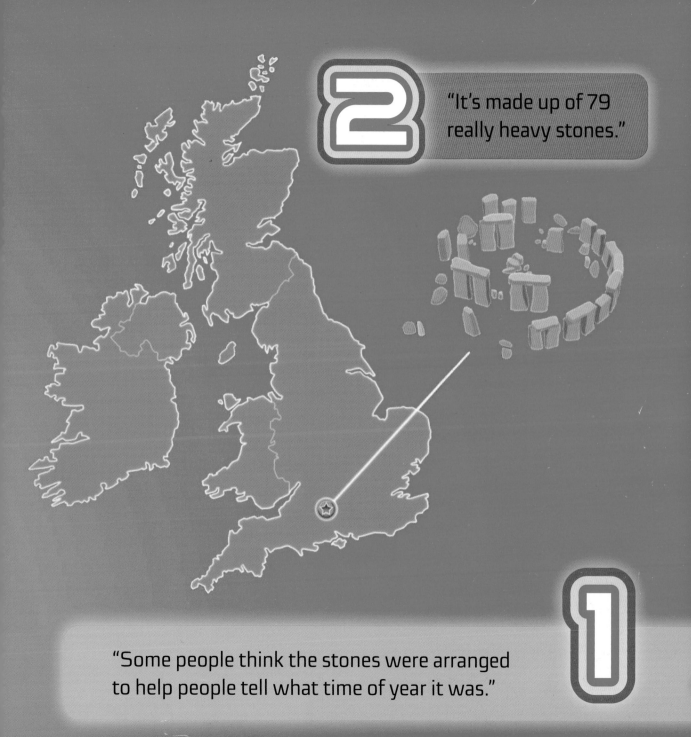

2 "It's made up of 79 really heavy stones."

1 "Some people think the stones were arranged to help people tell what time of year it was."

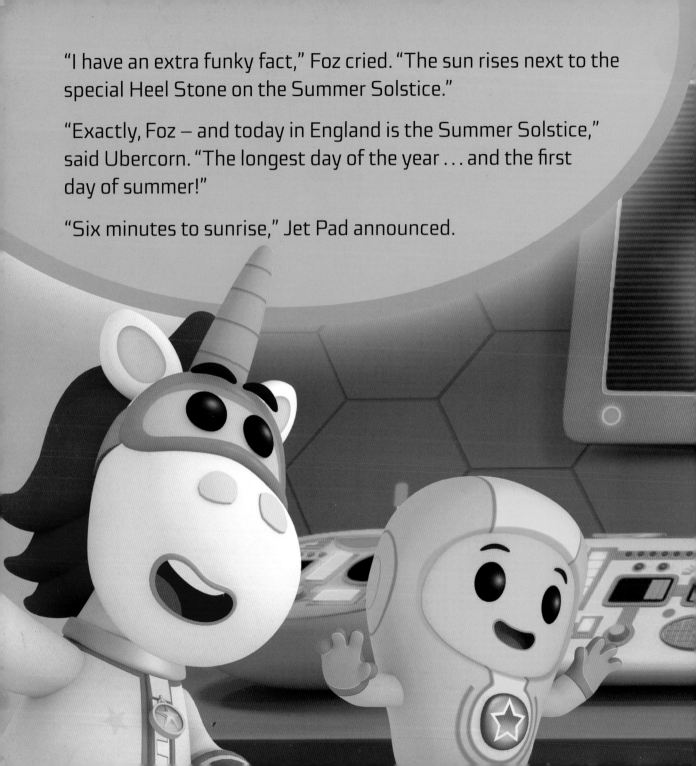

"I have an extra funky fact," Foz cried. "The sun rises next to the special Heel Stone on the Summer Solstice."

"Exactly, Foz – and today in England is the Summer Solstice," said Ubercorn. "The longest day of the year . . . and the first day of summer!"

"Six minutes to sunrise," Jet Pad announced.

The Go Jetters hovered above Stonehenge.
Lots of people were down by the stones, also
waiting to see the spectacular summer sunrise.

"Sunrise plus Stonehenge equals . . .
a dream come true," sighed Foz.
Suddenly, Xuli gasped.

"What was that?"

It was Grandmaster Glitch, knocking
down all the stones of Stonehenge.
He was trying to do a giant domino run!
"I'm going to need a run up!" Glitch cackled,
and sped his hover scooter towards
another stone.

"Get down there, Go Jetters, and save
Stonehenge!" said Ubercorn.
"To the Vroomster," called Xuli.

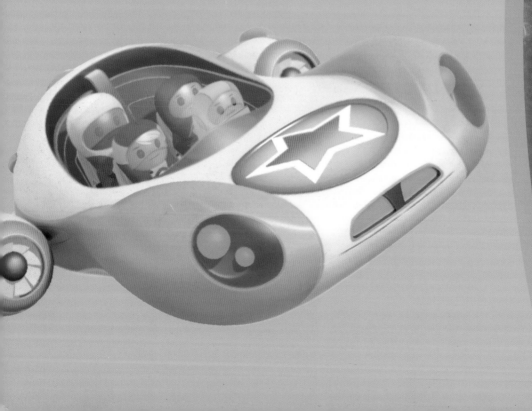

"Lars, Foz, get the stones standing again while Kyan and I stop Grandmaster Glitch!" said Xuli. She dropped them at the base of Stonehenge and swerved away.

But the stones were **too heavy** to move.

"We need click-ons!" Foz realized.
"Time for a mix to fix that glitch," Ubercorn agreed.

The quick-thinking unicorn picked out some gadgets, giving Foz a G.O. Giant and Lars a G.O. Ball. Then the Go Jetters hurried back towards the fallen stones.

Lars shot an energy bubble
under the first stone. As the
bubble got bigger and bigger,
it helped Foz lift the stone
back into place.
"Perfect," he grinned.

Meanwhile, Xuli and Kyan were chasing
Grandmaster Glitch.

Suddenly Kyan noticed that one of the
stones was about to fall on to a souvenir seller.
Just in time, he leapt to push her out of the way.

"Aced it!"

he shouted as the stone
came crashing down.

The sun was nearly up, and the Go Jetters got the last stone standing just in time ... but Grandmaster Glitch was gearing up for one last kick!
"Down you go, dominoes!" shouted Glitch as he zoomed forward.
"I have an idea!" said Foz, rushing to hold up one of the stones Glitch was about to kick.

Lars blasted an energy bubble between two more stones, just as Glitch drove into them at top speed . . .

... and bounced right back!

"Griiiiiiimblllllles!"

Glitch shouted angrily, as the force of the G.O. Ball shot him backwards into the sky.

"Great job, Go Jetters!" said Ubercorn. "And just in time for summer to start."

Together they watched the sun rise above the hill and shine over Stonehenge.
"Geographic!" said Lars.

"Sunrise selfie!" cried Xuli, snapping a photo before they headed back to Jet Pad.

Thanks to the Go Jetters, summer in England started without a hitch. Another successful mission – and who knows . . . maybe one day they'll zoom through the clouds above you!